DEMCO

The Mommy Book

TOdd PARR

Megan Tingley Books

LITTLE, BROWN AND COMPANY

New York ∾ Boston ∾ London

ALSO BY TODD PARR:

The Best Friends Book
The Daddy Book
The Family Book
The Feel Good Book
It's Okay To Be Different
Reading Makes You Feel Good
The Peace Book

For a complete list of titles and
more information about Todd Parr,
his Web site address is www.toddparr.com

Little, Brown and Company

Hachette Book Group USA
1271 Avenue of the Americas, New York, NY 10020
Visit our Web site at www.lb-kids.com

First Edition
Library of Congress Cataloging-in-Publication Data

Parr, Todd.
    The mommy book / by Todd Parr. — 1st ed.
     p. cm.
    "Megan Tingley Books"
    Summary: Represents a variety of mothers, with short hair and big hair,
driving minivans and motorcycles, swimming and dancing, and hugging and
kissing their children.
    ISBN 0-316-60827-0
    [1. Mothers — Fiction.] I. Title.
PZ7.P2447 Mo 2002
[E] — dc21   2001029098

10 9 8 7 6
TWP
Printed in Malaysia

This book is dedicated to
all the different kinds of moms
who have worked so hard to make
life a little bit easier with their
unconditional love and support.

Especially MY MOM!

Love,
Todd

Some mommies drive minivans

Some mommies drive motorcycles

Some
mommies
wear
jeans

Some
mommies
dress up

Some mommies make snow angels with you

All mommies like to

Some mommies like to dance

Some mommies work at home

Some mommies work in big buildings

Some mommies teach you how to paint

All mommies like to watch you sleep!

Some mommies have short hair

Some mommies have big hair

Some mommies
like to cook

Some mommies like to order pizza

Some mommies go fishing

Some mommies go shopping

All mommies love to kiss

and hug you!

Some mommies
fly kites

Some mommies fly planes

Some mommies sing you songs

Some mommies read you stories

All mommies want you
to be who you are!